MW01519601

Sparks From The Same Fire

By
jasdeep Singh

Cover Artwork By Simreet Kaur
esskaurdesign.com
Instagram: @esskaurdesign

ISBN: 978-1-7772709-0-2

Interior Design by booknook.biz

"Just as From One Fire Tens of
Millions of Sparks Arise
They Become Distinct
Then In the Fire They Meet"

Sahib Sri Guru Gobind Singh
Akaal Ustat
Sri Dasam Granth Sahib Ji

Contents

The Chaah is Boiling Over

A special thank you to those who inspired,
guided and reassured me in writing this story.

Amee Walia
Kiranpreet Rishi
Keisha Paterson
Jessica Rodrick

"Youth Goes Without Being Seen
Decay Arrives One Goes With Death"

Sahib Sri Guru Amar Das
Sri Guru Granth Sahib Aad Darbar Ji
1414

The Chaah is Boiling Over

The rain is coming down hard outside. It hits the basement window like repeated knocks, asking to be let in. But it's already inside. She feels it in the spaces where her bones meet. The cold dampness is already in her knees, her wrists, and the small of her back. She spends most of her days like this, sitting in the torn, but soft, grey armchair facing the small basement window. December skies in Brampton don't offer much excitement, but her soul gave up a long time ago, and now, she just needs something to pass the time.

The best way for her is to remember. Her bones are old, and it takes her too long to get out of bed or to walk across a room, but once, she used to outrun all the boys in her village. They would line up on the dirt road beside the fields, and they would run, and all of Punjab would become a blur as she left the boys behind and ran past the carts and bicycles. Even after the others had given up, she would keep running, all the way to her father. She would catch him and grab his palm as he came home from working in the fields. Her tiny hand could barely wrap around one of his huge, calloused fingers, and they would walk all the way home for the dinner her mother had made. Sitting with him on the munjee, she would sometimes break off a piece of roti, pick up some subjee, and feed it to him. Years later, when she told him her husband wanted to move to Canada, her father looked at her with the spring rains in his eyes and asked, "Who will feed me now?"

In Canada, instead of feeding her father, she would break off small pieces of roti and feed them to her husband. There was no munjee here, just a mattress on the floor, but it was enough for her. She would reassure him that if the companies he applied to wouldn't hire him because of his turban, then they didn't deserve to have a Sardar with them. "They don't know how to recognize a king."

The pain in her bones is too much today; she needs something to make her feel warm again. She feels weak, too weak to stand, but she tries. She finally succeeds and slowly walks over to the kitchen. Each step is heavy and painful. On her wedding day, her mother told her the gods in the sky were watching because they'd never seen someone so graceful. Her father told her the reds and yellows in the phulkaaree of her Punjabi suit made the sunset feel shy. Today, in this basement, with its water damage and black mould, she doesn't feel any of that grace.

She takes a pot sitting on the stove and brings it over to the sink. She fills it with enough water for two cups but then remembers there's only one person here. She's been alone for years now, ever since that night at the hospital—the overcrowded one on Bovaird—yet she still fills the pot with two cups worth, until she remembers. She pours out some of the water and places the pot on the stove. Her recipe hasn't changed in a lifetime. She'll add the tea bag and spices and wait for it to boil. She likes it to be strong, so she'll wait for a while before adding the milk. Then she'll wait until it almost boils over, but at the last moment, she'll take the pot off the stove. The chaah has boiled over only once in her entire life; that night she called the ambulance. While she was begging him to wake up, the tea was rising up and spilling out of the pot. At the same time, he was rising up and spilling out of his body.

She has enough energy to pour in the milk, but not enough to stand and wait for it to boil. So, she slowly walks back to the armchair. She'll come back soon, but until then, she needs a moment to rest. She won't let the chaah boil over.

Her breathing is heavy, her arms are sore. It feels like she's carrying someone on her back, but in reality, she carried an entire family on her back for years.

Her husband was always good to her. Despite double shifts at the security company, then years later, double shifts at the factory, he always stayed kind and gentle. So, she made sure that despite her own shifts at her own factory, she never let him go without his cup of chaah.

Sometimes, when he was getting ready, she would stand by the door of the bedroom with a full cup and watch him tie his turban. He would drape it over his shoulder, and the world could have been dying outside, but he would have died before he let the fabric of his kingship touch the ground. She does remember though, how his eyes had died a little the day their son came home without his own turban, and in its place, a modern haircut. Her husband hadn't said anything, but he was always a little less than whole after that day.

On the day their son was married, his father watched him run upstairs and throw the turban he was made to wear for the ceremony onto the dresser. It hit the top drawer and fell to the floor and partially underneath the dresser. His father slowly knelt down to pick it up, and when he stood up again, he dusted it off and softly said, "Priests and relatives gave you advice today, all I can say to you is that if you want to honour your father's turban, be good to your wife. It was who we were before we lowered ourselves to being average."

The rain is softer now. The knocks on the window aren't as frequent. It reminds her of the day they moved here, and her husband led her by the hand down the wet steps into this basement. Her son and his family visiting was a regular happiness for her then, but slowly, over time, the visits became less frequent, the phone calls were farther apart. It was raining the day he sat them down in the kitchen of the old house. They all had a cup of chaah in their hands. He waited for everyone to take a few sips before he slowly mentioned that they were moving to Oakville. "It's not that I don't like Brampton, I don't like all the brown people here. There's too many." She didn't understand—his skin, his eyes, even his nose—they all looked the same today as they did yesterday, but somehow, they were different now. It didn't matter; she was excited. She was proud. Her son had bought a house, he had a family, all their sacrifices were worth it. Instead of buying clothes for herself, she had paid for a tutor so he could pass math. Instead of going to sleep when she was tired, she had left food on the counter for him to eat when he came home. Instead of buying a ticket to go to her father's funeral, she had paid his tuition. It was all worth it. But his father was quiet. He waited for the rest.

"I've found a great basement for you. It's near the Gurdwara. Rent is cheap. Your pension should cover it."

He promised to bring the grandkids over all the time, and for a while, he did. For a while, he would call too. Eventually, the kids were always busy, he was busy. His cell phone reception wasn't very good, he was in a meeting, Oakville was far away. He didn't pick up when she called him from the hospital, but he picked up the next day when the doctor called and told him about the heart attack.

The rain has stopped, the chaah is starting to boil. She closes her eyes. She's lining up on the dirt road; now all of Punjab is a blur, the others have given up. She keeps running. The chaah is boiling over, but there's no one here to drink it.

The Man on the Curb

A special thank you to those that inspired,
guided and reassured me in writing this story.

Amee Walia
Kiranpreet Rishi
Tyler Duff
Brian Seng-Low
Keisha Paterson

"As You Know Yourself Know Others
Then Be a Partner in Paradise"

Bhagat Kabir Ji
Sri Guru Granth Sahib Aad Darbar Ji
480

The Man on the Curb

The man on the curb wraps his hands around the paper cup. He's trying to draw as much warmth from it as he can. He needs it right now. It's a cold night, it's a cold parking lot, and he feels a strange cold inside of him. The cold he feels isn't the kind that's measured in degrees. It's a different kind. It's the kind that crystalizes inside a person's soul. It freezes over emotions and turns someone into a tundra of isolation. This is a crowded city, but he's alone.

He's trying to decide if he should go to the hospital. Nothing feels broken, but he's got a bad cut under his eye and a few cuts on his arms. If he goes to the hospital, he'll probably be waiting for a while. For now, he's fine here.

The bus he had been waiting for just drove by. He didn't even look up, he just let it go. If it had been here 20 minutes ago, his night would have gone differently. Snow delays everything.

After they were gone, when he was alone, he sat for a while where they had left him. After a few minutes, he decided to get up and walk over to the coffee shop and order his tea.

"Do you need an ambulance?" the young woman behind the counter had asked. "I'm ok," was his soft response.

He always tried to be a little kinder to the people we treat as "extras" in the movie of life. A simple "how is your day going?" before he places his order or a "thank you for the ride" as he gets off the bus sometimes makes a difference in a person's day. Even though it hurt to talk, he tried his best to be thoughtful.

He didn't want to, but he forced himself to look up at the young woman behind the counter. Her skin was a soft, golden brown as if someone had decided to mix chocolate and honey and paint a person from the result. Her hair was the kind of black that flowed from the spaces between suns and stars. He wondered what it looked like when it wasn't neatly tied in a hair net. But her eyes were tired and overworked. It was apparent that her and sleep were casual acquaintances who didn't meet as often as they should have.

"How long have you been here for? You're studying?" he asked. She was surprised that someone was taking the time to talk to her. Especially someone with a bleeding lip and a boot print on his cheek. "One year so far. I study during the day and work here at night." "How do you like it?" "It's hard, studying all day, then working all night. But back home, there's no future. Too many drugs, too much corruption, too much pollution. No jobs. It's better here."

"Good luck with everything," he said with a smile as he walked out with his tea. Once outside, he decided to sit and think on the curb, but for some reason, the thoughts didn't come. The cold was beginning to freeze them. Slowly, on that curb, his mind started to shut down. All he could do was focus on the warmth of the paper cup.

Out of the corner of his eye, he sees someone walking towards him. At first, he thinks they've come back, but it's just one person. The stranger walks over but doesn't sit down. There's silence except for the sound of slush from a car that's passing on the road. The man on the curb doesn't look up, but he knows the stranger is studying him. Looking him up and down.

The stranger begins to speak and asks, "How many were there?" The man on the curb keeps staring at the paper cup. He watches as the steam dances out of the opening in the plastic lid. "Seven, I think."

The stranger looks at him, "I'm guessing they jumped you because of your beard and turban? Because you're a Sikh?" There's that silence again. The man on the curb wants to answer, but he doesn't know how. It's like his mind is a car with a dead battery. He's trying to get it to start, but the ignition just won't turn. Finally, he stops trying to answer the question; he stops trying to make sense of what happened. Instead, he looks up for the first time.

Now it's the stranger's turn to be studied. Clothes. Face. Right eye. Without notice, the man on the curb has a realization. His mouth is now able to put words together as he looks at the stranger. He wants to be thoughtful, so he pauses for a moment and says, "I don't want to make an assumption about you—" The stranger cuts him off, "They probably jumped me because I'm a man wearing makeup and a dress."

Something happens in that moment—a calm understanding. They both know what happened to each other. The stranger replies, "What'd they scream at you?" The man on the curb replies, "Terrorist, what about you?" The stranger doesn't want to answer. His bruised eye will heal, but that word they used as they casually walked away has been seared into him over and over again since he was little. The hurt it causes won't go away.

"I was waiting for the bus. What about you?"

"I got a flat tire. I got out of the car and was trying to call my boyfriend when a fist came out of nowhere. I was on the ground, but as they were walking away, I counted seven."

There's no more steam dancing out of the paper cup. Instead, snowflakes are landing on the plastic lid. The man on the curb thinks for a moment, then tries standing up. It's a slower process than usual. The dull pain in his body has been replaced with an exhausting stiffness. Once the process is complete and he's on his feet, he turns to the stranger and smiles. "I'll help you change your tire."

"Ok, but then I'll drive you to the hospital. We'll be waiting for a while, but we can fill the time by seeing what else we have in common."

The Pipeline Man

A special thank you to those that inspired,
guided and reassured me in writing this story.

Harry Snowboy, Cree Elder
Amee Walia
Kiranpreet Rishi
Davinder Singh Sidhu
Jasmeet Sikand
Heather
Sophia Lazarus
Christine Head
Nicole Wolny

"Air is the Teacher Water is the Father
Mother is the Great Earth
Day and Night are Two Nurses,
in Whose Lap Plays the Entire World
Good Actions and Bad Actions are
Read in the Presence of Virtue
Based on One's Actions,
Some Are Close, Some are Far"

Sahib Sri Guru Nanak
Jap Ji Sahib
Sri Guru Granth Sahib Aad Darbar Ji
8

The Pipeline Man

The quiet man sat on a cold mahogany piano bench next to a stroller. His eyes began to fill as he looked down. He had bought the grand piano for her—the rarest wood, the most intricate craftsmanship, the best money could buy. When he had found out she would be arriving soon, he began daydreaming about listening to her play for him when she got older. He imagined driving her to practice, then to recitals. Finally, one day, she would be playing in a theatre in front of an awestruck audience. His eyes continued to fill as he thought about daydreams that would never come true.

Every night before he took his sleeping pills—the strongest he could find—he believed his eyes couldn't water anymore. How could they? How many tears could one man hold? But the next day, when he would turn over and look at the crib beside his bed, when he would rise and see his newborn daughter, the levees in his eyes would break, and his cheeks would flood. He wanted everything for her. He was willing to give her everything. Now, all he could do was listen as she used up the last few breaths she had been given in this life.

He put his hand in the stroller and let her grasp his finger. The tears streaming down his cheeks flowed into the smile his lips made when she kicked her feet.

Occasionally, his eyes would turn from her, to the ventilator attached to the side of the stroller. He used to think of the tubes as snakes, but now, he thought of them as branches. They weren't injecting poison; they were delivering life.

He wrinkled his nose and made the face she liked. She giggled under her breathing mask. He could see the faint outline of her smile through the translucent plastic. He had gotten used to the mask, but the scars on her chest were the hardest to look at. He knew what was underneath. When the team of doctors had told him that her lungs had been destroyed, the only option was to open her up and put in new lungs—lungs that were partially grown in a lab and partially assembled in a factory.

He stood up and gently grasped the handlebar of the stroller and paused for a moment as he looked into her eyes. They were her mother's eyes. The same eyes that he had fallen in love with so many years ago. Whenever he had looked into his wife's eyes, he would tell her how beautiful they were, how deep, how strong, how they made him think of things greater than himself. She would reply, "These are my ancestors' eyes. I see the world with their strength and their pain."

He thought back to the first time he saw those eyes. The first time he saw the woman to whom he decided to give every ounce of his soul. She was on the front page of a newspaper. Her hair was matted, and her clothes were drenched from the police water cannons. There were dark bruises on her arms and face from the rubber bullets and police batons that had been let loose on the lines of peaceful protesters. Even with pepper spray in them, those eyes were fierce. They were determined. "Protesters Continue to Block Pipeline on Indigenous Land," the headline had read.

When hundreds of billions of dollars worth of oil and gas were discovered on treaty lands, the government had tried to use legal manoeuvres to force Indigenous nations to give up their land rights. In the end, it was just an insidious way to eliminate Indigenous land sovereignty, which had been seen as an obstacle to development since colonization. Various nations were told to weigh the sacredness of the Earth against the much-needed revenue that drilling and mining could bring. History began to repeat itself when it became clear that corporations and governments would benefit, and Indigenous people would continue to be deceived and robbed.

Clean energy advocates argued that oil was archaic. The sun, wind, and water could provide more than enough energy, and investment in renewable energy would create more jobs and heal the Earth. But petroleum propaganda was a python. It coiled itself around the people, and lobby groups successfully swallowed any detractors by funding political campaigns and buying politicians. Indigenous people were the ones who suffered the most from the constriction.

The quiet man's mind travelled back in time, thinking about everything that had happened. He thought to himself, "If only the world had respected Indigenous wisdom, maybe we could have saved ourselves. Instead, they were mocked with Halloween costumes and sports team logos."

Years later, for some strange reason, fate decided to be kind to him. The same woman was in another newspaper. This time, she was in a dilapidated makeshift hospital at a refugee camp. She was suffering from the sickness that had taken so many lives. Just like the generations before her, she was displaced. Her home had been stolen. The land that her family had lived on for thousands of years was taken away.

As soon as he had seen her picture, he called in all his favours, used as much money as was needed and had medicine and supplies delivered to the camp. They called him a hero. They said he must have saved thousands of lives. Hers was one of them.

He helped her recover and pretended to be someone he wasn't. The more he deceived her, the more they fell in love, until one day, he became her husband.

His daughter's eyes began to close. Whenever she would close them, he would look at the monitor on the ventilator, wondering if she would ever open them again. As she fell asleep, he began pushing the stroller. The rubber wheels rolled over the dark wooden floors of the living room, making a soft sound.

The sounds of the ventilator echoed off the walls of his colossal home. The breeze from the industrial air purifier system felt cold against his skin. He hated the hum the old unit had made, but he had to tolerate it. Any unfiltered air from the outside would be fatal. Eventually, he used his money and influence to get a quieter system developed. Now, the silence in his home was haunting. His footsteps echoed, the ventilator echoed and the screams of his past echoed.

He continued pushing the stroller through the hallway at a slow pace. Each step tired him. His legs were heavy, and his hands could barely produce the grip needed to hold onto the handlebar. His feet moved slowly as he dragged them across the floor in black dress shoes that had cost more than most people in the world earned in a lifetime. His perfectly tailored black pants and fitted white dress shirt were no less expensive. His clothes were once a status symbol; now they were like dead skin hanging from a corpse. It was strange how they matched his surroundings as he moved along. There was so little colour around him. The stroller rolled over dark marble floors that were contrasted with stark, white walls. The quiet man no longer noticed the rare art and artifacts he was walking past. Things that had once drawn crowds in the world's most famous museums were worthless to him. Punjabi thrones made of gold, Egyptian hieroglyphs, European paintings, and a few sculptures were, to him, no different than the things found at the bottom of a garbage can. When the food riots had destroyed almost every city in the world, he had gathered these things with arrogance and pride. Now, the mountain of wealth he had created couldn't fill the empty cave inside of him.

At the end of the hallway was a stone arch, where the black hallway marble turned into precisely laid grey brick. The sound of the moving stroller changed as it left the marble and rolled over the path. Today, just like most days, he was taking his daughter for a walk through the indoor forest. He had paid so much for this forest. It was one of the few that remained in the world; most plant life had died off quickly when the sunlight was partially blocked out. But in this place, inside his home, redwoods hundreds of feet high grew beside roses, jasmine flowers, lavender, hydrangeas, orchids, cherry blossoms and hundreds of varieties he didn't know. His favourite was the pool of lotuses, where he would take the stroller and find a bench to sit on. The calm water would bring calmness to him as he thought about all the things he had done. Sometimes, when the quiet of the forest was too much for him, he would turn on the waterfall and watch the water cascade 200 feet down into the pool below. The sound of the water blocked out the sound of the ventilator, and for a moment, the noise blocked out the noise in his head. He continued pushing the stroller slowly, making his way to the spot where he would rest—the lotus pool at the base of the waterfall.

His wife had loved the water. She fought so hard her entire life to protect it, but no matter how determined she was, clean water slowly disappeared. Oil spills from tankers and pipelines became more common. Water tables around the world continued to drop, and finally, wars for whatever was left escalated until the only drinking water available was from expensive filtration systems that only the rich could afford. When the oil and water wars destroyed infrastructure, North Americans and Europeans learned what it meant to walk miles for drinking water like people in other parts of the world had been doing for generations.

It was ironic, he supposed, that when the ice melted, the storms and floods had destroyed and submerged half the world. Shanghai, Hong Kong, Miami, Mumbai, New York, and New Orleans were a few, but eventually, dozens, then hundreds of cities around the world began drowning. Hundreds of millions of people were displaced; trillions of dollars were lost. The world had assumed there was time. Warnings from scientists were ignored, but when the sea levels began to rise faster than expected, when the storms became stronger and stronger, time had finally run out. There was too much water, but when it came to clean drinking water, there wasn't enough.

Water wars became as familiar as oil wars, and as the dust from new types of chemical weapons mixed with exhaust fumes, earth, water, and finally air were turned into poison.

He had this forest built for his wife to keep her mind away from the reality that existed outside. But she had never forgotten. She would come here every day and rest in a place that couldn't exist outside. Despite all its beauty, this was where the last bit of her heart had been broken.

He tried his best not to think about the day he had told her everything. Those beautiful eyes, the horror in them, then the rage. Everything she knew was a lie. When she had screamed and run out, he didn't try to stop her. He had been sure she would return quickly. The battery on her suit was not full; she couldn't stay out very long. But when she hadn't come back, worry spread in him like an infection deep inside his soul. Later, at the police station, the officer began writing a missing persons report, but that one word in her description had made him put away his pen with a sigh. He had pointed to a box full of folders filled with reports containing that word.

The stroller reached the lotus pool now. The quiet man angled it beside a wooden bench and let out a soft sigh as he sat down. Looking into the stroller, he thought about that one word—how it flowed through his daughter's veins just like it had flowed through her mother's. His wife would tell him about it and the history of pain it carried. "Indigenous," she had said. "Indigenous women and girls have been disappearing for generations. The media talks about it once in a while, but Indigenous people live with it every hour of every day. The police have boxes filled with files and walls covered with pictures, but when it comes to solutions, there's nothing."

He hadn't understood until now, until the moment he was filling out a report for a missing Indigenous woman. When the police couldn't provide him with any real answers, he left, and he understood the same fear and frustration an entire people had felt for years.

But the quiet man had money and resources, and he used them to quickly assemble his own search teams. The image of her when he found her kept him up at night, and strong pills were his only escape from the waking world. But more often than not, he couldn't distinguish between the nightmares he saw when his eyes were closed, and the ones he remembered when his eyes were open.

He had found the deserted back alley where she had gone into labour early. He had found her mask and suit, the same mask and suit she had taken off and put on her newborn daughter. A mother's sacrifice, giving her own life to protect a new life. But the battery had been weak, and the filter couldn't keep all the particles out of her daughter's lungs. He found them both. For his wife, it was too late, but for his little girl, the frantic drive to the hospital had come in time, and the doctors were able to save her. They were able to keep her alive, but when they had used their sophisticated machines to assess the damage, they realized that all they could do was delay the inevitable. In that moment, the result of a lifetime of greed was staring at him from a neonatal incubator.

For years his wife had suspected something but wasn't sure what. Whenever she spoke about oil companies and pipelines, he remained quiet, and so, she began calling him, "The Quiet Man." She would talk about the protests she had gone to. He remembered her lips when she would talk about the oligarchy that was ripping the world in half. "Don't these people have a heart? Do they not believe in a Creator or God?"

He would imagine what his lips might have looked like when he finally broke his silence and told her, "Power is the only God; money is its priest."

Had he been wrong?

He, of course, had been raised in a world of wealth and luxury; she was the granddaughter of a residential school survivor. He had been given the best tutors, the gentlest care from a family full of every kind of privilege one can imagine. She had inherited intergenerational trauma. "Colonialism," she often said, when she was teaching him about the real world, "Colonialists sailed around the world and raped everything they could find for their benefit, and the governments that followed continued what had been started earlier. Instead of songs and stories, instead of language and culture, pain and despair are passed down from generation to generation—from parent to child." The peculiar thing was, whenever she spoke, there was no despair in her eyes. He would ask her why, and her reply would always be the same. "I remember who I am." When she would say it, there was lightning in her eyes. "As long as a people remember who they are, they will never stop fighting for their rights. Power rests with those that control the narrative."

He knew exactly what she meant. Controlling the narrative was how he had insidiously achieved his objectives, but he pretended not to understand, so she had to explain it to him. "The dominant narrative is what shapes the views of the average person."

He made a confused look, so she explained further. "When Indigenous people fight for their rights, they are vilified. When people of African Ancestors fight for their rights, they are vilified. When Sikhs fight for their rights, they are vilified. Savages. Criminals. Terrorists. Each human rights movement is given a label. Some journalists are paid or threatened by corporations and governments to create a narrative of lies and xenophobia towards each group, towards the oppressed. But when the oppressed take control of the narrative, the shackles on their wrists will turn to dust in storms of resistance."

She would continue, "Indigenous People, People of African Ancestors, Sikh People—all people who stand up against injustice. Resistance and revolution are intertwined within their DNA. The outcome has been determined."

He had quietly asked, "What is the outcome?"

She had smiled at his question as if the answer was obvious. "Freedom." It was obvious to her. "But first, pain. First tragedy. Then freedom, and from freedom, restoration. When dying languages will be green again like a forest after the rain. When dried-up cultures will overflow like rivers at their banks. Freedom."

She would often sit on this bench, holding her belly, singing to the future that was growing inside. "This song," she would explain, "it's sacred. My grandfather taught it to me." As the ancient words drifted through the trees, she would tell his story.

"Grandfather had been playing as a child when men he didn't recognize stole him from his family. They took him to a residential school. It was one of many schools created by the government and the churches to isolate Indigenous children from their families and assimilate them by destroying their culture and beliefs."

She would inhale, close her eyes, then exhale and continue, "The sacredness of his hair was cut away from his head, the wisdom of his language was cut away from his tongue, and the beauty in his heritage was cut away from his soul. Everything he loved was ridiculed as they tried to 'kill the Indian in the child' and 'get rid of the Indian problem.' Psychological. Emotional. Physical. Sexual. A cultural genocide built on every kind of abuse imaginable," she would say.

She would stop, and reflect, then continue. "Pain had been sewn into his sinews with thread made of despair. But he endured. Unlike so many other children—he survived," she would say as she gazed down at her belly. "Grandfather was a survivor of the school, and when he left, something inside of him rekindled. He began learning; he began planning. He planned for his future, but also for those to come. And he reconnected. They had tried to destroy his heritage, but it only fuelled him to fall in love even more. He turned every drop of pain into an ocean of love for his people, and when I was old enough, he shared that love with me."

"The first time I saw him in his regalia," she whispered, "he looked at me and said, 'This is who you are. You are from philosophers and warriors. You are from intellectuals and artists. You are from astronomers and healers. You are from explorers and inventors. But most of all, you are from courage and resilience.'"

He now sat on the same bench where, finally, he had told her everything. She had accidentally found his old documents and confronted him. The fragrance of the jasmine flowers slowly spread over him like it had that day. He had sat motionless, staring at a lotus. They say a lotus grows in dirty water but lives above it. He had hoped that the two of them could live above the dirt of his past, so finally, after a long silence, he turned to her and tried to cleanse his soul.

When an executive from an electric car company had announced that new technology was about to make gasoline obsolete, oil prices plummeted. Oil company board members and the governments of oil-producing countries had held an emergency meeting. The quiet man was given a task. He manipulated the media to undermine the electric car company's objectives. False reports about the company's reliability shook shareholder confidence, and gossip was circulated to destroy the executive's reputation. In the end, it was ineffective. The executive was determined to save the world. He worked day and night, and because of his passion, cars were built and sold, clean technology continued to be developed, and it looked like there might be hope.

The executive had organized a drive from Los Angeles to New York to prove the technology was reliable and practical.

The quiet man was asked to take a more persuasive approach. The electric car could drive itself, but it couldn't make food; so one night, when the executive had pulled over for some dinner, the team that the quiet man had hired planted something underneath the car. Later, the world watched, through a livestream, as the executive's vehicle erupted into a blaze. They listened to his screams and the crackling of the flames. Almost overnight, electric car technology was abandoned, and oil prices soared. Billions were reinvested in oil exploration and extraction, and that created new problems for the industry. Much of the new oil had to be drilled on or transported through Indigenous treaty land. The protests erupted as compromised politicians tried their best to justify it, but nothing could placate the people. First Peoples from all over the continent galvanized, and the support of the general public grew.

The industry held another meeting, and the quiet man was given a new task. That oil had to be extracted at any cost; those pipelines had to be built. They named him "The Pipeline Man."

He had researched for hours, then days, but no solution presented itself. "December 29, 1890. Wounded Knee," he read. "The massacre of innocent and unarmed Natives during sacred ceremonies." No, he couldn't do that. Massacring innocent Indigenous people was what governments had done for centuries, but he needed something less obvious. Then, he realized that the solution already existed. It had existed for centuries; it just needed a little updating. Genetic engineering had advanced immensely, and that technology was available to him. He set his plan in motion; a new type of virus would be manufactured, which would target specific elements of Indigenous DNA. Early settlers used gunpowder and germs to solve their Native problem. Today, The Pipeline Man would only need germs.

The new virus was released, and slowly, the people who cared about the earth, sky and water faded away. Treaty lands were annexed, Mother Earth's veins were replaced with steel tubes, and every single article in the United Nations Declaration on the Rights of Indigenous Peoples was ignored.

Propaganda campaigns were relaunched with bribed scientists and politicians who claimed environmental degradation was a hoax. Industry lobby groups lulled the world's population with false assurances; with those assurances, industry boomed and men in positions of power became richer. Millionaires made billions, billionaires made tens of billions and the average person lost everything. When the world realized what happened, it was too late. Life expectancies dropped rapidly. The average person died at 70, then 60, then 30. Hundreds of millions began to disappear. He had started it all.

As he spoke, her new reality drifted into her like a fog. The truth slowly blocked her throat and swirled in her lungs until she could barely breathe. He knew then that there was too much dirt in the pond for the lotus to grow. Slowly, gradually, her breath, which until then had disappeared, began to deepen. She started to breathe faster, stronger; through her nostrils, she expelled what love she thought she had for him as her body began to shake. Generations of pain poured out of her eyes and down her cheeks. Centuries of betrayal strangled her as she tried to scream. He stood up to hold her, but she pushed him back onto the bench and ran. There wasn't time for anything else. There wasn't time to think, there wasn't time to breathe, there wasn't time to check the battery on the suit she grabbed from the hallway before she was gone. The Pipeline Man was left in stillness except for an artificial breeze that moved through the branches hundreds of feet above him.

That same breeze moved through those same branches now. The lights that created an artificial sun began to change colour. The manufactured sunset wasn't as beautiful as the real ones had been—he knew the difference. Humanity had tried to control everything, but his wife had told him once, "There is a sacredness inside everything natural, and no matter how accomplished Man's ego becomes, that sanctity cannot be recreated with circuit boards."

Before the world had been destroyed, how many people, he wondered, had appreciated their inhales and exhales? How many people had truly tasted the water they drank? How many people had ever put their bare feet in the soil?

The pool of water reflected the deep orange and yellow light as the sun began to set. The Pipeline Man continued looking at his daughter. She opened her eyes one last time, and then slowly closed them. It was her last gift to him. Her last reminder that, in the infinity of time, every moment is sacred. That thought and action are two lovers who give birth to the future, and the intention of those lovers, in the moment of their union, will shape the world.

He watched her inhale and exhale. How simple, but so beautiful; the soft rising and falling had captivated him for hours every day these past few weeks. This forest had become a theatre, he was the awestruck audience, and her life was a sonata.

The monitor began to beep as her chest slowly stopped expanding. When she was completely still, he turned off the ventilator and took off her mask. He cradled her and carried her to the place he had prepared weeks ago. As he held her in his arms for the last time, he silently recited a prayer her mother had taught him. He asked her ancestors and the Creator to reunite his daughter with the mother she had never known. As the rays from the artificial sun grew stronger, he lowered his daughter into the earth and slowly began filling it with soil. He wanted to use his hands; he wanted to feel the earth with his palms. When the soil was used up and the mound complete, he made his way to his feet and took two steps to the left and fell to his knees in front of an older, larger mound of dirt. He silently asked the woman who had her ancestors' eyes for forgiveness. He told her that her daughter was coming to be with her.

The Pipeline Man stood up and inhaled the crisp, clean air deeply—something he realized most of the world hadn't been able to do for years.

As the final artificial rays dwindled, an artificial moon appeared in the sky. Pale light blanketed the forest and the two mounds of dirt. Familiar shapes became unfamiliar shadows. Tall trees and flowers became ghosts in a jury, and the forest became a courtroom. The evidence had been presented, the sentence delivered, and the guilty prepared.

The Pipeline Man made his way to the ventilator and turned it on. In the stillness, he wanted to listen to it one last time. He walked to the pond and gently stepped into the water. He took out the plastic bottle that he had kept in his pocket every day for the past few weeks and removed the white safety lid. When he had thought about this moment every day, he had assumed he would be terrified, but now that the moment had arrived, as he looked at the pills in his hand, standing knee-deep in the pond, he was calm. He gently brought his palm to his mouth and placed the pills under his tongue. He waited for them to dissolve, and once they had, he turned around and sat down in the water facing the two mounds. He knew that he deserved worse than this; he knew that soft and painless wasn't what most of the world had been given. As his eyes closed and before his head slipped under, the sound of the ventilator echoed.

Blessed Me, Mother of the World

A special thank you to those who inspired,
guided and reassured me in writing this story.

Amee Walia
Kiranpreet Rishi
Davinder Singh Sidhu
Gaia Oakhem
Mallika Kaur
Harsimar Singh
Baghael Kaur
JPK
Himmat Singh Khalsa

"Cosmic Realms Universes Without End
Giver of Salvation Your glory Is Yours Alone
My True Beloved"

Sahib Sri Guru Arjan
Sri Guru Granth Sahib Aad Darbar Ji
963

Blessed Me, Mother of the World

The young woman ran barefoot down the steps. The cold, white marble that was common in upper-middle-class Delhi homes was smooth against her bare feet as she walked into the family room. She walked over to the couch where her grandparents were seated and kissed them. First, she kissed her grandfather's forehead, then her grandmother's. Foreheads with wrinkles and scars. Wrinkles and scars are like sentences and paragraphs that tell the biography of our lives in languages we often forget to read. Every morning, when she kissed her grandparents, her lips read her lineage. Her history. Her identity.

The television was on. Her grandparents were watching a loud preacher wave his hands while delivering holier than thou speeches. She listened for a moment, then walked away with an annoyed look on her face. She walked into the kitchen where her brother was washing dishes, and her parents were sitting sipping tea. Her father gently broke a biscuit in half and dipped it in his mug. He waited as it slowly drank up the tea, and when it seemed that the biscuit was close to dissolving, he removed it from the mug and took a bite. Her mother removed her mouth from her own mug after a slow sip, leaving red lipstick on the brim. The young woman gave her mother a kiss and her father a hug, took a bite of the toast they had buttered for her, and together they all turned towards the family room to sit with her grandparents.

She was a paradox—a system of thoughts and beliefs that seemed to contradict themselves but aligned so perfectly within her. When she walked up and down her college campus, her steps flowed with the elegance of a midday breeze. But when she was angry, her words beat down like the midday sun. Her professors were amazed at how quickly her mind put things together but were even more astonished by the juxtaposition of her warm nature with her vicious courage. Her hands were soft, but she knew how to curl her manicured fingernails into tight fists. While her friends were adamant about proving how drunk they could get, she didn't judge them. But instead of joining them, she enjoyed the integrity of old hymns that filled her with a different kind of inebriation. What was interesting was that instead of ostracism, her resolve garnered her respect and love from those around her.

Nosey people with no hobbies and too much time would ask her grandfather why his granddaughter was such a strange mix of the new ways and the old ways. He would reply, "A remarkable woman is like a beautiful rose—both have many petals, but people have fallen into the habit of plucking them." Her grandfather would then laugh and continue, "If I told you that I would not let you tear apart my granddaughter because she is who she wants to be, it would not matter. What matters is that my granddaughter will not let you tear her apart. Our people have never been in the business of raising meek women. We teach our daughters about women who led men into battle. One thing was asked of them—become great warriors. Mentally. Physically. Spiritually. These traditions are one reason we have survived for so long."

With that, the people with no hobbies and too much time would reply with the most indignant snort and change the topic.

The young woman stood in the rays of sun that streamed through the family room windows. Specs of dust suspended in the sunlight circled her like stars around the centre of a galaxy. She took a wooden comb from her pocket and undid the bun her long hair had been tied up in. Her hair flowed down her back like a river of defiance as she tilted her head to one side and put the comb to use. Her hands moved gently, and the wooden comb did its work.

Centuries ago, when the invaders had come to this place and turned it into a city of corpses, the people had screamed for their lives. They had begged the holy men who littered every corner for help. The holy men had prayed to their idols, their gods, their heavens, but no idol, no god, no heaven had heard the screams—no invader had lost his sight.

The invaders would sip at the souls of the people for centuries, and no one stood up until the world was introduced to the ones whose hair flowed down their backs like a river of defiance. Around the world, long hair was the right of the strong. In this place, it was the sworn identification of those who protected the ones that could not protect themselves.

In this country, the people had made sacred the rivers that flowed near their cities. But no river was more sacred than the one which sprang from the young woman's scalp and flowed down her back and to her hips like courage flows down the eyes of a commoner to his lips. It was those commoners that had prayed to the only goddess left, and with her blessings in their hands, their courage swelled at its banks and flooded the countryside with sacrifice and compassion. The invaders starved with broken spines and broken empires. Rivers sustain cities, but the river that flowed down her back had freed nations.

Every stroke of the young woman's comb through that river was a tribute, a prayer to a people that had left a long time ago. Betrayed by their own and the ones they had freed, they went away from this place, promising to return one day.

The young woman's attention was suddenly drawn to the words of the television preacher. "He couldn't have written it. It is all a lie. What mother are they talking about? It's a lie."

The young woman remembered growing up in a place different from here. She used to run to school and see old men with white beards and tall blue turbans sitting under trees tending to horses. She would steal every spare moment she could find to sit with them and listen to their prayers. She remembered something they would say, "Blessed Me, Mother of the World." One day, an old man with a powerful presence had turned to her and explained something, "She isn't what they think she is. She represents the qualities we ask for. The things we beg for before battle. When we beg for her blessings, we are begging for courage, for strength. When we had her blessings in our hands, we brought freedom to this place. Today, the old ways are forgotten, and people sleep with chains around their necks. It is too difficult for them to believe that divinity can be expressed as a woman."

The young woman thought for a moment, and then he continued. His eyes were looking at something she couldn't see; they were remembering someone the rest had forgotten. His voice became soft and quiet. "Many stood beside him, even more, stood behind him. But only we stood in front of him, praying that every arrow and bullet that was meant for him would come rest in our chests, and all we asked in return was that when he looked at us, his eyes would say, 'You are my beloveds.' For us, he sacrificed his blue horse, his white hawk, his mother, his father, his four sons, his cities, even his shoes—everything. He sacrificed everything for us."

After that day, wherever the young woman went, she silently sang the prayer she had been taught, "Blessed Me, Mother of the World."

She tied her river back into a messy bun, grabbed her bag and began her walk to her college.

It was a typical day in Delhi. Pollution filled her nostrils as she navigated the broken streets that corrupt politicians had promised to fix. She walked this way every day—the same stray dogs, the same naked children. Both dogs and children starving, neither understanding the wealth that government thugs enjoyed. The young woman walked and thought and, as always, sang her prayer under her breath, "Blessed Me, Mother of the World."

"This place could be so beautiful," she thought. "The people are strong and resilient. They built cities and practiced art and science when most of the world was in the dark. But they've been robbed too many times."

Her thoughts were interrupted by calls for, "Mango shake! Mango shake! Delicious! Delicious! Mango shake! Mango shake!" The calls were coming from a little boy whose father had been selling mango shakes out of the same cart for ten years. One day, a group of men had felt that a "low caste" should not sell food, and so they had decided to educate him on the traditions of caste boundaries. That education ended with a newly widowed woman wondering how she was going to feed her children. The little boy had gone back to the spot where his father had been beaten and decided to carry on the "delicious mango shake" anthem.

The young woman and little boy would spend a few minutes conversing each day as he poured her a shake. Sometimes, she would silently contemplate the strength a 9-year-old needed to stand each day in the place where his father had been murdered, just so that his mother could buy her children some stale rice. His clothes were old and torn, his sandals broken. He couldn't speak English, and he couldn't afford to watch the latest movies. But there was more hero in him than the film stars, cricket players or fashion models this country adored.

Once she had finished her mango shake, she continued walking, but the coolness of the shake was a short reprieve from the heat of the day. The day was hot because the fire of corruption burns hottest at its base. This city was that base. The young woman was soon sweating. Her thoughts drifted, and she imagined how beautiful a breeze, cool like justice, would feel on her face. Moments later, the leaves on an ancient tree rustled, and the strands of hair on the back of her head moved in the wind. But the breeze hadn't come from the sky. She looked over, down a dirty alley, deserted and forgotten. At the end of the alley stood an old door. Faded black wood with brass inlays, the door was an ancient remnant in a modern city. She had never seen it before. She had never seen the building before, even though she walked this way every day. She was late for college, but she couldn't move. She just looked at the entrance of the building. Her soul was like a scrap of metal being pulled by a magnet, and she walked down the alley, past the door, through the threshold, and into an empty room.

The room was dark and cold, with obvious signs of antiquity. Why was she here? Why couldn't she leave? She soon realized that she was talking out loud; her prayer once again left her lips. "Blessed Me, Mother of the World."

Suddenly the young woman turned around and realized she wasn't alone. In front of her stood an old man. He stood over a head taller than the average man, with marks on his face where blades in combat had blessed him. He wore a blue gown that ended at his thighs and was fastened by blue fabric wrapped around his waist. Tucked in the fabric were a sword, a mace, and more blades. Iron bracelets encircled his wrists to mid-forearm. He wore long white cotton undershorts and a tall blue turban. She looked at him, and then his turban, and it seemed like it climbed up past the sky away from the Earth to swirling galaxies that travelled around it like pilgrims seeking divinity. His eyes were calm, like a clear sky, and his beard was like the clouds missing from it. In his eyes were safety and peace. In his eyes, prayers were being sung, and naked children were being clothed. In his eyes, beggars were being fed, and those who could not walk were now dancing.

And the young woman blinked.

And he was gone, but in his place stood a woman. She wore the same clothing. Her skin seemed like it had been painted by the elements with earth as colour and sun as brush. The young woman looked into the other woman's eyes. In her eyes, infants were being born, and universes were collapsing in on themselves. In her eyes, the monsoon was pouring, and the sandstorm was screaming. In her eyes, everything that ever was and ever will be existed together. It seemed as if she didn't sustain herself with air, but instead, her lungs took in lightning, and the current flowed through her capillaries to her muscles. The by-product returned through her veins, back to her lungs, up her throat, and when her lips parted, they released courage and sacrifice, justice and devotion.

And the young woman blinked.

She looked around; she was in Delhi. But it wasn't the Delhi she knew. The suffocating pollution had vanished from the air. The room was lit brightly; the door seemed new. She made her way to the threshold and looked out. What time was this? What place was this? Soldiers in chainmail lined the streets with broken spears and abandoned swords at their feet. The city gates were open. The city had gates? Outside the gates, dust climbed into the sky like a people's prayer, but the storm that raised it was a people's rebellion. Men on horses rode in, but not just men. Women were riding too. Their blue turbans scraped the sky, sending sparks of freedom to the earth, where infernos ignited and engulfed corruption and greed, leaving the charred embers of persecution. They wore swords that reflected the sun so brightly, even the moon bowed its head in reverence.

And the young woman blinked.

She was on a hill, somewhere far away in a place surrounded by lush fields and dense forests, where five rivers brought life to brittle people. The people had named the rivers, but the young woman somehow knew them by other names. Compassion. Righteousness. Courage. Unwavering. Master. She looked around. She was surrounded by an ocean, dark and deep with no end. Her eyes adjusted, and she realized it was an ocean of people like the riders in blue. Each one of them was like a wave rising. Millions of waves, with hundreds of thousands of horses. They held battle standards, too many to count—triangles of greyish-blue cloth that had more light than a thousand stars when they fluttered in the breeze. Somehow, the young woman felt something she had no way of knowing. This ocean around her had flooded the shores of tyranny and hate; it had drowned intolerance and fear. Wherever its water ran, peace, understanding, and equity were nourished.

And the young woman blinked.

She was back in the dark room with the old door. The old man and the other woman stood in front of her. They were there, but they weren't there. Their energies had merged but remained distinct. They were one, but unique. The young woman was confused. She understood they were more of a feeling, not actual corporeal existence. Without her realizing, her lips released her prayer, "Blessed Me, Mother of the World." As soon as the air around her had snatched the words from her breath, the old man and woman extended their arm and placed something in the young woman's hand. She felt it. She knew it. It was the goddess that had heard the people's prayer. The only idol, the only divinity that had stopped the torrents of grief that had swept the innocent away, was now in her hand.

And the young woman blinked.

When her eyes opened, she was alone in the old room with the old door. The rancid Delhi air attacked her lungs, and she began to cough violently. Maybe she had fainted or lost her mind. Maybe something, maybe anything, could explain what had just happened. Until she realized her hand still held the gift she had been given. She lifted her shirt and tucked her goddess into the waistband of her jeans. She suddenly wondered how much time had passed and quickly raced to college.

She was a few minutes from the entrance to campus when she stopped. In her haste, she had forgotten to run to the entrance she normally used. The problem? With this entrance, she had to walk by a tea shop. The problem? They would be sitting on the steps, enjoying glasses filled with India's favourite past time. Slow sips. Waiting. Waiting for women from the college to walk by. Waiting to call out, waiting to gesture, waiting to intimidate. Waiting to make themselves feel powerful. She took a deep breath, paused, then started to walk. She tried not to look, but she felt their gaze, a gaze that burrowed itself underneath her skin and spread like an infestation. Her throat became dry, and her heart began to beat faster. The beats seemed to align with her steps. One beat. One Step. One Beat. One Step. Then she heard them call out to her. She tried not to look. "Don't look. Please don't look at them," she pleaded with herself. Then the comments started. She stopped. Her childhood prayer was on her lips. "Blessed Me, Mother of the World." A cold ferocity slowly spread over her. Her body was porous as she absorbed courage—courage that coated her insides—filling and sealing every empty place she knew. Today was not the day she was going to be afraid. She looked at them. Some wore collared shirts with haircuts like Bollywood actors. One had a sweat-stained white undershirt. Dress shoes. Running shoes. Sandals. Jeans. Shorts. Dress pants. They sat on the dirty concrete steps in front of the teashop. Their smiles quickly disappeared as they saw the vicious look in her eyes. When she was a child, she had been told by the men with white beards and tall blue turbans that when a tiger is surrounded by jungle dogs, she pounces and kills their leader first. The other dogs usually shrink away in fear.

She walked up to him—the one who had made the comments. The one with the sweat-stained white undershirt. She picked up the glass of tea in front of him, held it in her hand for a moment, then threw the liquid at him. There were now new stains on his shirt to go along with the old ones. She took a step back, then casually dropped the glass from her hand, letting it shatter on the concrete by his feet. He didn't make a sound. She looked around. No other jungle dog looked her in the eye. They had tried to tie her down with their gaze. Suffocate her with their stares. Now, just a few minutes later, they didn't have the courage to even look up at her. She turned around and went to her college.

The day passed in confusion and agony. She didn't understand what had happened in the alley, and her mind would not stop repeating the same words. The same prayer. It was as if those words had become her breath, and to survive, she needed to inhale and exhale them. But somehow, every lesson that was taught in class that day was easily understood and mastered.

It was dark when she began her walk home. She often stayed to help tutor her friends, but today, she hadn't realized how late it was. The sun had run away, and the streets were dimly lit by dilapidated streetlights surrounded by thousands of mosquitoes. The young woman felt uneasy as she listened to the sounds of her sandals on the concrete. Governments all over the world had issued warnings to female tourists about the dangers of walking alone in this country. The young woman soon realized the mistake she had made when she had lost track of time.

She quickened her pace and tried to conceal her anxiety. As she walked faster, her surroundings grew more ominous. Doors were closed, and the shops were deserted. She turned a corner to walk down an alley connecting two major roads. Before she realized that the light from the street was afraid to follow her, strong hands grabbed her and dragged her into the dark. She screamed, but the walls of this city had listened to men and women screaming for centuries, and they, like the people who lived here, were accustomed to the sound.

The young woman kicked and fought desperately, but she only found herself thrown to the ground. She looked up at him. His sweat-stained white undershirt couldn't contain his belly, and his eyes couldn't contain his intent. He walked forward with the vicious belief that he was entitled to her. The young woman screamed, "The police will find you!" But his reply silenced her, "The police are concerned with finding the most bills for their pockets." He took another step towards her. "This is your fault. What respectable girl stays out so late? If you were respectable, this wouldn't happen." It wasn't about respect. It was about power. She had made him look and feel weak. He wanted to be strong.

She tried to turn and run, but she was disoriented and soon realized that her back was to an unforgiving brick wall, and an overflowing dumpster stood guard on her left side. He blocked her on the right. She was sweating, she was pleading, she was terrified. She tried to run past him, but he tripped her, and she fell hard, and her hopes for escape, escaped like the air in her lungs.

He was on her before she could react. His hands became manacles around her wrists that declared her his captive. He shifted his weight and moved his left hand to her neck. She gasped and tried to scream, but air was a dwindling commodity in her throat, and she felt her energy drain away. As her eyes began to dim, she did what she had done since she was little. She whispered her prayer,

"Blessed Me, Mother of the World."

Suddenly her thoughts shifted from the certainty of her fate to a realization. He was holding her hand down, and his other hand was squeezing the life out of her. But she had a free hand. She struggled, but he matched her by shifting his weight again. She fought and gasped for breath and then fought some more until her free hand moved across her and began searching. Her hand searched for the goddess that she had tucked into the waistband of her jeans. The young woman found her, gripped her softly with her fingers, and her goddess moved like a melody across the man's belly. Elegant and subtle, she danced, and the world paused in reverence.

The man with the sweat-stained white undershirt awoke to the realization that he was leaning against an unforgiving brick wall with an overflowing dumpster to his left. He looked down at his stained undershirt. Sweat stains, tea stains, and now red stains. In the dim light, he realized that the organs that had once been in his belly were now in his lap. There was a puddle around him when there hadn't been one before. His hands were resting on his thighs, and they were drenched in something he did not know.

The world was quiet, and his confusion increased when he realized that other than him, everything was still. He looked down at the other end of the alley he was lying in, and in the distance, he noticed that the swarm of mosquitoes around a lone streetlight was not moving. It was as if air had turned to glass and everything inside it was suspended. There was no sound, no movement, nothing but a pause. And the stillness was broken by something he registered in his periphery. They stood there, dark and unwavering, terrifying but tranquil. Three of them, each in a cloak and cowl. They drifted towards him until they stood in front of him. The mosquitoes were still prisoners in their suspension. The stranger in front was flanked by his counterparts, and as he came closer, from inside his cloak emerged a staff held by a silent hand. The silence carried forward as the staff moved like a shadow and struck the man on his head. He tried to scream, but air no longer existed to reverberate his terror. They began to drag him away, and he couldn't stop them.

The man kicked and fought desperately, but it was no use. They continued to pull him across the ground, and as they dragged him away, a calm fascination came over him. His gaze was caught by something at the mouth of the alley. There stood an old man. He stood over a head taller than the average man. A few steps away from him stood a woman. Her skin seemed like it had been painted by the elements with earth as colour and sun as brush. In between them stood a young woman with a river of defiance flowing from her scalp down her back to her hips.

Something in her hand reflected the light from the street. The metal was sharp, and the blade was wet with bits of things that had once been in the man's belly. No idol, no god, no heaven had heard the young woman's scream. But when the edge of her goddess had moved across his belly, he had been opened up, and she had been saved.

The young woman's lips moved as the man was dragged away. And for what seemed like the first time, he was able to hear something. He heard her childhood prayer, and the pause ended.

Manufactured by Amazon.ca
Bolton, ON